*To my children and all those who believe in unicorns – AD*
*To my children, Clare and Max – JB*

Picture Window Books are published by Capstone,
1710 Roe Crest Drive, North Mankato, Minnesota 56003
www.mycapstone.com

**Library of Congress Cataloging-in-Publication Data**
Names: Darlison, Aleesah, author. | Brailsford, Jill, illustrator.
Title: Ellabeth's test / by Aleesah Darlison; [Jill Brailsford, illustrator].
Description: North Mankato, Minnesota: Picture Window Books, an imprint of
    Capstone Press, [2017] | Series: Unicorn Riders | Summary: When Willow
    breaks her leg, Ellabeth must step into the role of Head Unicorn Rider as
    the remaining three riders set off on a dangerous mission to obtain
    diamonds from the Dakkar serpent, who must give them up willingly—but
    Ellabeth is not sure she has the courage or judgment to lead the way,
    especially after she insults the serpent.
Identifiers: LCCN 2016007995| ISBN 9781479565474 (library binding) |
    ISBN 9781479565559 (paperback) | ISBN 9781479584864 (ebook (pdf))
Subjects: LCSH: Unicorns—Juvenile fiction. | Magic—Juvenile fiction. |
    Animals, Mythical—Juvenile fiction. | Courage—Juvenile fiction. |
    Responsibility—Juvenile fiction. | Adventure stories. | CYAC:
    Unicorns—Fiction. | Magic—Fiction. | Animals, Mythical—Fiction. |
    Courage—Fiction. | Responsibility—Fiction. | Adventure and
    adventurers—Fiction. | GSAFD: Adventure fiction.
Classification: LCC PZ7.1.D333 El 2017 | DDC 813.6—dc23
LC record available at http://lccn.loc.gov/2016007995

Editor: Nikki Potts
Designer: Bobbie Nuytten
Art Director: Nathan Gassman
Production Specialist: Katy LaVigne
The illustrations in this book were created by Jill Brailsford.

Cover design by Walker Books Australia Pty Ltd
Cover images: Rider, symbol and unicorns © Gillian Brailsford 2011;
lined paper © iStockphoto.com/Imageegaml;
parchment © iStockphoto.com/Peter Zelei

The illustrations for this book were created with black pen,
pencil, and digital media.

Design Element: Shutterstock: Slanapotam

Printed and bound in China.
009959S17

# UNICORN RIDERS

# Ellabeth's Test

Aleesah Darlison

Illustrations by
Jill Brailsford

PICTURE WINDOW BOOKS
a capstone imprint

# Willow & Obecky

### Willow's symbol
- a violet—represents being watchful and faithful

### Uniform color
- green

### Unicorn
- Obecky has a black opal horn.
- She has the gifts of healing and strength.

# Ellabeth & Fayza

### Ellabeth's symbol
- a hummingbird—represents energy, persistence, and loyalty

### Uniform color
- red

### Unicorn
- Fayza has an orange topaz horn.
- She has the gift of speed and can also light the dark with her golden magic.

# Quinn & Ula

### Quinn's symbol
- a butterfly—represents change and lightness

### Uniform color
- blue

### Unicorn
- Ula has a ruby horn.
- She has the gift of speaking with Quinn using mind-messages.
- She can also sense danger.

# Krystal & Estrella

### Krystal's symbol
- a diamond—represents perfection, wisdom, and beauty

### Uniform color
- purple

### Unicorn
- Estrella has a pearl horn.
- She has the gift of enchantment.

# The
# Unicorn Riders' World

Kingdom of Obeera

Kingdom of Lillius

Kingdom of Korsitaan

Maylee

Trope

Mountains of Trope

Sea of Desperation

Trilby

Kingdom of Avamay

Palace

UR Compound

Effervescent Falls

City of Keydell

Desperation Point

Stillmet

Tivia Wood

Cardamon

Miramar

Arlen

Hot Springs

Islands of Ipsus

Merroweed

Gringot

Woods of Shanahan

Lake Feather-Jay

Dove Mountain

Kingdom of Haartsfeld

Gulf of Curzon

Dagger Mountains

Idle Bay

Sea of Angels

# The Unicorn Riders of Avamay

Under the guidance of their leader, Jala, the Unicorn Riders and their magical unicorns protect the Kingdom of Avamay from the threats of evil Lord Valerian.

Decades ago, Lord Valerian forcefully took over the neighboring kingdom of Obeera. He began capturing every magical creature across the eight kingdoms. Luckily, King Perry saved four of Avamay's unicorns. He asked the unicorns to help protect Avamay. And that's when ordinary girls were chosen to be the first Unicorn Riders.

A Rider is chosen when her name and likeness appear in The Choosing Book, which is guarded by Jala. It holds the details of all the past, present, and future Riders. No one can see who the future Riders will be until it is time for a new Rider to be chosen. Only then will The Choosing Book display her details.

# • CHAPTER 1 •

ELLABETH STOOD IN THE center of the pavilion whirling her fighting stick high above her head. With lightning speed she brought it down to strike the training mannequin.

"Kee-ha!" she cried, hitting the mannequin again.

Ellabeth loved her self-defense classes. It had taken years of discipline and training to learn these special skills. She had worked hard to perfect her moves.

Before becoming a Unicorn Rider and moving to Keydell, Ellabeth had lived in Cardamon, among banana groves, mango trees, watermelon patches, and cornfields. Her father was a farmer, and her family lived in a small wooden house on stilts. They didn't have much, but one thing her father had taught her was martial arts. Her father, mother, and five younger sisters had always encouraged Ellabeth and taken her to compete at local tournaments where she had excelled.

"Well done, Ellabeth," said Jala, the Unicorn Riders' leader. "Accurate and controlled as always. Now, let's see your hand-to-hand moves."

Ellabeth put her stick away and then stepped onto the padded floor of the training ring. She faced Jala with her body held firm in the warrior stance. Her knees were slightly bent and her hands were raised flat and straight in front of her.

*Find a gap in your opponent's defense,* her father's voice spoke in her mind.

Ellabeth advanced. She struck at Jala with her hands and her feet, trying to make contact with each movement.

Jala was a master of martial arts, but Ellabeth hoped that if she focused her mind and controlled her movements, she might defeat Jala. Just this once.

The other Unicorn Riders, Willow, Quinn, and Krystal, sat cross-legged outside the training ring, watching Jala and Ellabeth. They had already had their turn against Jala and had failed. It was up to Ellabeth now.

Ellabeth wasn't as tall or as strong as Jala, but she was agile and had quick reflexes. Now, as she advanced on Jala, she did as her father had taught her. She watched her opponent's eyes, reading for a sign of what she would do next.

For a second, Jala hesitated. Ellabeth saw her opening. She rushed in to strike, but made a costly

error by leaving herself unprotected. Jala took full advantage, knocking Ellabeth skillfully to the mat.

Ellabeth lay on the floor staring at the ceiling.

"Almost had me," Jala said, grinning as she leaned over Ellabeth.

"Almost isn't good enough," Ellabeth groaned with disappointment. "I really wanted to win this time."

"That's what you always say," Jala said as she hauled Ellabeth to her feet. "Perhaps next time."

Ellabeth straightened her uniform. She plucked a stray thread from the hummingbird symbol embroidered on the front. Every Unicorn Rider had her own unique symbol that represented her personality. Like the hummingbird, Ellabeth was bursting with energy. She rarely sat still. "Can't I try again? Please?" Ellabeth begged.

Jala squeezed Ellabeth's shoulder. "Enough for now," she said. "You push yourself too hard."

"Hey, you were great," Willow, the Head Rider, said as she patted Ellabeth on the back. "Terrific moves."

"Very impressive," Quinn agreed. "Jala's impossible to beat!"

"You did way better than us," Krystal added.

Ellabeth blushed at her friends' praise, secretly delighting in it. Their praise helped her forget her frustration.

*I'm so lucky to be a Unicorn Rider and to call these girls my friends,* she thought.

Ellabeth still remembered how hard it had been leaving her family to become a Unicorn Rider. Having the other girls around had made it much

easier. She had quickly fit in, and although she still missed her family sometimes, she truly loved being a Unicorn Rider.

Back to her old self, Ellabeth smirked. "Well, I did better than you at least, huh, Krystal?" Ellabeth said.

"Honestly," Krystal said shaking her head, pretending to be offended. "I don't know why I bother sometimes."

"Ha! You just can't handle the truth," Ellabeth teased.

The two girls were well known for their friendly teasing. Everyone laughed, Jala included.

As the other Riders bustled her out of the pavilion, Ellabeth promised Jala, "One day I'll surprise you, Jala. Just wait and see."

Jala smiled. "Ellabeth, you surprise me every day!" she said.

# • CHAPTER 2 •

THE GIRLS WERE IN the stables getting their unicorns settled in for the evening. Fall was giving way to winter, and the weather was growing colder. Already there had been snow, causing temperatures to drop.

Ellabeth was making sure her unicorn, Fayza, had enough water to drink. Quinn was feeding Ula a treat of green apples, while Willow broke apart fresh clover hay for Obecky. Krystal liked her unicorn, Estrella, to always look her best and was braiding her silky mane.

A bell clanged up at the main building of the Unicorn Riders' estate.

"Sounds like Jala wants us," Willow said.

"Maybe it's a message from the Queen," Ellabeth suggested.

The Unicorn Riders often went on missions for their Majesty, Queen Heart. Sometimes their missions were to battle Lord Valerian, the evil ruler of Obeera to the north of Avamay. Other times the Riders helped people in danger. There was always something exciting happening for the Riders and their unicorns.

"Let's go see," Ellabeth said.

The girls raced out of the stables. The sleet had made the courtyard icy and slippery. Willow slid and fell, landing awkwardly on the bricks.

"Willow! Are you all right?" the Riders exclaimed as they gathered around her.

Willow clutched her shin. "My leg!" she moaned.

Ellabeth and Quinn slung Willow's arms over their shoulders and helped her back into the stables.

"I'll get Jala," Krystal said, before running off.

Moments later, Jala came running.

"Is it broken?" Willow asked. She panted in pain as Jala examined her leg.

"I'm afraid so," Jala replied.

"Can Obecky heal it?" Quinn asked.

"Obecky's magic can relieve the pain and help with the healing," Jala explained, "but I still have to set the leg properly."

Ellabeth let Obecky out of her stall. The unicorn nickered softly, clearly upset that her Rider was in pain. She sent a shower of gray-blue magical sparks out of her horn and over Willow's leg.

"Ah, that's better," Willow said as her face slowly regained color. "I am so glad Obecky has the power to ease pain."

"Let's get you to the hospital so I can set that break," Jala said.

"What about the bell?" Ellabeth asked. "Is there a message from the Queen?"

"Yes," Jala said. "Her messenger is waiting for us. We'll get Willow settled, and then we'll meet with him."

"Can't Obecky just heal the break?" Willow asked. "That way I can come, too."

"No," Jala said firmly. "A broken leg can't be taken lightly. It must be set the old-fashioned way. Otherwise, you'll never walk properly again."

Willow nodded sadly. She didn't argue further.

The Riders helped Willow to the hospital, leaving Alda, the housekeeper, to fuss over her while they headed to the meeting room.

The queen's messenger was waiting for them, dressed in his purple uniform and gold sash.

"Honorable Riders," he said. He bowed as he handed Jala a letter carrying the queen's waxed seal, a dancing unicorn.

Jala carefully broke the seal and opened the letter.

She took a breath and started reading the letter to the Riders.

Dear Riders,

Avamayan tradition decrees that when a young royal turns twelve, he or she must begin military strategy classes, starting with an initiation ceremony. Princess Serafina's initiation ceremony will take place in three days, and the Unicorn Riders' role in it is crucial.

The Dakkar Diamonds should be collected and brought to the palace so Princess Serafina's magical armor can be made. The diamonds, which are actually the scales from the Dakkar Serpent, have to be fresh and given freely by the serpent, otherwise their magic will die.

In these dangerous times, the Princess needs her magical armor more than ever. As I write this, Lord Valerian's forces threaten our borders from the north. Great battles lay ahead.

I beg you, dear Riders, travel to Dakkar immediately and secure the diamonds. Avamay is depending on you.

Yours,

Queen Heart

"The Dakkar Diamonds," Ellabeth gasped. "I've heard about them."

"It's been over three decades since they were needed," Jala said. "The last initiation ceremony was for Queen Heart herself."

"This is my kind of mission," Krystal said. "Loads of diamonds and zero danger."

"It sure will be an adventure," Quinn agreed.

"Don't underestimate this mission," Jala said. Her warning cut through the room like ice. "I've never been to Dakkar, but I've heard it can be a treacherous journey. Trust me, this isn't a fun ride to collect pretty diamonds."

She gazed out the window at the drifting snow. "Not only will you have to battle the weather, you must race against the clock to reach Dakkar," Jala said. She turned back to study the Riders with a grim smile. "They say the place is protected by the black Mists of Shanahan. Few have ever dared to enter the forest. I don't know a single person who has come out of there alive. And when, or if, you arrive at Dakkar, you must also convince the serpent to give you her scales."

Ellabeth felt a shiver run down her spine. If Jala was trying to scare them, she was doing an excellent job.

*I must be brave,* Ellabeth thought. *This mission is important.*

"Nothing will stop us," Ellabeth said. Her voice came out sounding sure and steady, though her hands trembled. "We'll do it for Avamay."

"I'm glad to hear it," Jala said, her worry lines relaxing slightly. "As Queen Heart warned, Lord Valerian's troops are forming on our northern border. The Council of Kingdoms will be held in a few short weeks, and you will accompany Queen Heart and Princess Serafina there. The princess must take part in the discussions. If a peaceful solution can't be reached, the eight kingdoms may be plunged into war. Princess Serafina will have to actively help in the defense of her country."

"But the princess is such a shy little thing," Krystal said. "How can she be expected to do all that?"

"Because one day she will be a queen," Jala said. "*Our* queen." Jala caught each Rider's eye. "So you see, this will be a great test for you all. You don't have much time, and Avamay's future rests in your hands."

The Unicorn Riders nodded solemnly. "We understand," they said in unison.

"Right," Jala said. "Then go prepare."

"What about Willow?" Quinn asked.

"Willow must rest while her leg heals," Jala explained. "I'm afraid you'll have to go without her."

"But we always ride as one," Quinn said.

"That's right," Krystal agreed.

"I'll lead," Ellabeth offered. She looked at the others expectantly, waiting for their response.

*I know I'm not as experienced as Willow,* she thought, *but I'll try my best.*

Krystal's eyes bulged in surprise. "You can't take Willow's place," she scoffed.

"I didn't mean I'd *replace* Willow," Ellabeth said. As she spoke, she felt her cheeks grow hot. "But someone has to lead the mission."

"I'd make a better Head Rider than you," Krystal said. "Besides, diamonds are my symbol." She pointed to the diamond embroidered on her purple uniform. "It must be a sign."

"Your diamond symbol isn't any better than my hummingbird," Ellabeth countered.

Krystal appealed to Jala. "Come on, Jala, pick me," she said.

*No,* Ellabeth thought, *pick me.*

"Quinn?" Jala asked studying the red-haired girl.

"I don't want to be Head Rider," Quinn said. She was adamant. "I'm happy letting someone else lead."

The more she thought about it, the more Ellabeth wanted to lead the mission. She adored Willow and was completely loyal to her, but she had always secretly wished to one day be Head Rider. This would be good training for her. Imagine how proud her father would be!

"Ellabeth?" Jala asked, interrupting her thoughts.

"Yes?" said Ellabeth.

"Can you lead this mission?" asked Jala.

"I sure can," replied Ellabeth.

# • CHAPTER 3 •

ELLABETH STOOD IN THE courtyard with Jala and the others, preparing to leave.

"I have something for you," Jala said as she handed Ellabeth a heavy object. Shaped like a hairbrush, it was round at one end with a long, narrow golden handle set with delicate orange topazes, the same color as Ula's horn.

"It's beautiful," said Ellabeth. She flipped the object over, trying to figure out what it was.

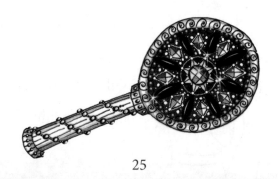

"It's a porta-viewer," Jala explained. She clicked a button on the side and slid the top open, revealing a circle of glass beneath.

"It looks like a mirror," Ellabeth said.

"It's very pretty," Krystal said.

Jala pressed another button. The glass misted and then cleared. Willow gazed out at them.

"Oh!" Ellabeth gasped. "It's magic."

"The image is so clear," Quinn said.

"I can see and hear you perfectly," Willow said from her bed in the hospital. "Can you hear me?"

"Yes," Ellabeth replied. She looked at Jala. "What's it for?" she asked.

"I thought it would be useful for you to talk to

 Willow now and then," said Jala. "That way you'll have Willow's support when you need it, and Willow won't feel so bad being left behind."

26

Ellabeth couldn't help feeling down. She had been chosen to lead the mission. Now she felt like Jala didn't believe in her. She wanted to say she didn't need Willow's advice or the porta-viewer. But she knew Jala was only trying to help.

"Keep in touch," Willow said. "I should go now. My leg's hurting again."

Ellabeth saw that her friend's face was pale and pinched with pain. "Okay," said Ellabeth. "You concentrate on getting better."

She clicked the porta-viewer closed and then stored it in her backpack. Nimbly, she leaped up onto Fayza. Quinn and Krystal also mounted their unicorns.

"Do we ride as one?" Ellabeth asked. It felt strange saying the words Willow usually said.

"We ride as one," Krystal and Quinn replied.

Ellabeth reveled in riding Fayza bareback, with only a blanket beneath her to help keep Fayza warm. No bridle, no saddle — just total freedom. Still, it was cold, and she had to pull her hood up to keep warm. Like the other Riders, she wore a thick woolen coat, gloves, and snow boots to ward off the freezing wind.

Night descended. The snow fell more thickly, and it grew bitterly cold. Ellabeth led the way on Fayza. Golden light shone from the unicorn's orange topaz horn, illuminating the night for the others to follow. Although Fayza's light made it easier to see, the cold and the snow drained the unicorns and the girls of their energy.

Despite the weather, Ellabeth couldn't help feeling excited that for the first time ever, she was leading the others as Head Rider.

*I hope I don't fail this mission,* Ellabeth thought as they plodded along. *I can't let Princess Serafina down.*

They came to a road that was rocky and slippery from the snowfall. The unicorns had to slow to a walk and carefully made their way along a narrow path snaking through foothills. The snow never let up. It made every step seem so hard. The girls rode in silence, intent on staying alert.

Eventually, they saw buttery squares of light calling to them through the darkness. A town lay ahead — Gringot.

"We should find an inn and ask if they have rooms for the night," Quinn said.

"I'd love to rest and get warm, too," Ellabeth said. "But we have so little time. We only have three days to make it to Dakkar and back."

"The snow's falling too thickly," Krystal reasoned. "We could put the unicorns and ourselves in danger if we continue on."

"Perhaps Fayza can double her magic so it warms us as well as lights the way," Ellabeth suggested.

"That will exhaust her," Krystal pointed out. "We don't want her magic weakened this early in the journey."

"What would Willow do?" Quinn asked.

"Maybe you could use the porta-viewer to ask her," Krystal suggested.

Ellabeth's stomach flipped. *Why couldn't they believe in her like they believed in Willow?*

"Can you please just trust me?" Ellabeth asked. "I'm Head Rider now. I know what's best." They had reached Gringot and were trotting through the streets. "We'll stop at this inn to ask for directions and a hot meal. After that we continue on."

"As you wish, *master*," Krystal teased.

"Hey, no fair," Ellabeth said.

"Well, you are being a bossy boots," Krystal muttered.

"Come on, you two," Quinn said calmly. "Don't fight."

She bit her lip, frowning. She knew Krystal was jealous that Jala hadn't pick her to be Head Rider. Ellabeth would just have to prove to Krystal that she could do this.

# • CHAPTER 4 •

ELLABETH LED THE WEARY Riders into the Gringot Inn. After making sure the unicorns were safely stabled, she and the others hurried inside. They found the place warm and empty except for three people sitting at a corner table.

"May we have a hot meal?" Ellabeth asked the innkeeper.

"Sure. Sure," The innkeeper said smiling. "Will meat pies and veggies do, Honorable Riders?"

"Yes. Thank you," replied Ellabeth.

As the Riders sat down, a slender woman with wild, knotted hair and unnaturally pale blue eyes entered the inn. The woman scanned the room for a moment and then strode up to the Riders. She tapped the table to get their attention. "I see it," she said. "It's here with us now."

"What is?" Ellabeth asked suspiciously.

"Death," the woman croaked. "Surrounding all of you!" She stabbed her finger at the Riders.

Ellabeth's hand trembled. Krystal and Quinn looked uncertain. "What do you mean?" Ellabeth asked. "Don't you know who we are?"

"That I do," the woman said, "and I have bad news for you. I've seen it written in the bones."

A chill swept up Ellabeth's spine. "B-bones?" she said. She hated anything to do with cemeteries or skeletons. Her fear went back to a terrifying night when she had been lost in a cemetery before she had become a Unicorn Rider. It was a night that had haunted her ever since.

The woman opened her hand to reveal several small, white bones.

They were animal bones, Ellabeth realized with a shudder.

"Come," the woman said. She motioned to the door as the innkeeper returned carrying plates of steaming hot food. "I have private things to tell you. You can hear me speak next door." She rattled her bones dramatically at them.

"Now, now, Delphi. Enough of that," the innkeeper warned her. "You go home. The Riders want to eat in peace."

Delphi refused to leave. She began to argue with the innkeeper.

"I don't think we should listen to her," Krystal whispered while Delphi was distracted.

"She seems so certain, though," Quinn replied. "Even if she is a little strange."

"More like a *lot* strange," Krystal murmured.

Ellabeth caught Delphi's attention. "I'm sorry," she said. "We've only stopped for a meal and to ask the way to Dakkar. We're in a hurry and can't stay."

"I know the way to Dakkar," Delphi said. "After you've eaten, come next door to see me." She held her finger up. "If you value your lives."

Delphi left, slamming the door behind her.

"Don't mind Delphi," the innkeeper said. "She's been through a lot."

Ellabeth hid her shaking hands beneath the table. She didn't want the others to see how upset she was. "Is it true she knows the way to Dakkar?" Ellabeth asked.

The innkeeper nodded gravely. "Dakkar is a peculiar, hidden place, protected by dark magic," he said. "As far as I know, the only way in is through the woods of Shanahan. Delphi spent years there, searching for her lost husband. Poor soul, she never found him. They say he was taken by the black mist that swarms through the woods."

Ellabeth exchanged glances with Krystal and Quinn.

"You'd do well to steer clear of Shanahan," the innkeeper continued, "otherwise you might end up like Delphi."

"I wish it were that easy," Ellabeth murmured.

The innkeeper left them to their meals.

"What does Ula think?" Ellabeth asked Quinn. "Is Delphi right about death surrounding us? Can she sense anything?"

Ula's special skill was sharing mind-messages with her Rider. She also had a knack for sensing danger before anyone else.

"I'll ask her," Quinn said. She fell silent while she communicated with her unicorn. "Ula sees black," she said eventually. "Lots of it. Things are quite blurry, but she does see Delphi helping us."

"Fine," Ellabeth said. "After we eat, we'll go see Delphi."

"I'm not sure about this," Krystal said. "Why don't you use the porta-viewer to ask what Willow thinks?"

"We don't need to bother Willow," Ellabeth said. "I'm in charge, and I think we should speak with Delphi."

"All right," the others agreed.

They finished their meal then went next door. The wind cut through Ellabeth's coat as she stomped through the snow to Delphi's cottage. Pale candlelight from the front windows cast ghostly shadows, and bones were tied together in an eerie wreath pinned to the door. These didn't look like animal bones.

"I can't go in there!" Ellabeth said frozen at the gate.

Quinn and Krystal stopped to stare at her.

"But you're Head Rider," Quinn said. "You should lead the way."

"Even if you don't like something," Krystal prodded.

*Thanks for reminding me,* Ellabeth thought.

Ellabeth chewed her lip, feeling trapped. She knew

 that as Header Rider she should lead the others, but her fear ran too deep.

"I can't go inside," said Ellabeth. "It's too creepy. Can you go without me?"

Quinn gently squeezed Ellabeth's arm. "Sure," she said. "If you're scared, it's best you stay here."

Ellabeth smiled to show her thanks. She didn't have the courage to look at Krystal. She was afraid she might see disappointment in the other girl's eyes, and she couldn't bear that.

Quinn knocked on the door. Delphi appeared and ushered her and Krystal inside. Ellabeth waited, jiggling her legs and blowing on her hands to keep warm.

*What are they talking about?* she wondered. *If only I had the courage to go in.*

After what seemed like ages, Krystal and Quinn returned looking worried.

"Well?" Ellabeth asked, searching their faces.

"We asked her to read her bones again. She foresaw trouble for us in the woods," Quinn explained. "She said we'll become hopelessly lost, and a terrible fate will befall one of us."

"Who?" Ellabeth asked.

"She couldn't say," Krystal said.

"She explained how to get to Shanahan," Quinn continued, "but she insisted we don't go through the woods to reach Dakkar. Instead, we should take the narrow path that skirts the woods near the town of Merroweed, where the dark magic is weakest. She said our only hope for survival is if we take that path."

"Merroweed?" Ellabeth said frowning. "That's miles to the west. It'll take ages to reach it in this weather, even with the unicorns."

Quinn shrugged. "She was certain we shouldn't go through the woods," she said.

"I don't know what good that advice is," Ellabeth sighed. "If we're to make it back to Keydell in time, we can't avoid Shanahan. Simple."

"Weren't you listening?" Krystal asked. "It's too dangerous."

"As Head Rider I have final say," Ellabeth said. She tried to sound firm so Krystal wouldn't continue to argue. "And I say we go through Shanahan."

# • CHAPTER 5 •

THE GIRLS RODE ON through the night. Ellabeth continued to worry over her decision about entering the woods.

*Have I made the right choice?* she wondered. *Will something terrible happen to us there?*

The thought made her feel sick.

"Please, Ellabeth, can we stop and rest?" Krystal asked. Her question broke Ellabeth's thoughts. "I'm exhausted and so are the unicorns."

"No," Ellabeth said. "We must press on."

"Why are you being so stubborn?" asked Krystal.

"Because we can't afford to fail this mission," Ellabeth replied. "You heard what Queen Heart said in her letter. Avamay is depending on us."

"Exactly," Krystal said. "Which is all the more reason to travel wisely and safely. If we keep riding like we are through this weather, we'll just end up getting sick."

"Please, Krystal, can't you just believe in me?" Ellabeth shouted above the howling wind. "You never argue with Willow like this."

"Because she doesn't make us do foolish and impossible things," Krystal said.

"Look!" Quinn shouted. She pointed at a dark shape ahead. "Perhaps we can shelter in that cottage. A few hours of sleep won't hurt," Quinn said. "And Krystal's right. We have to look after ourselves."

Grumbling under her breath, Ellabeth finally gave in. She hated admitting it, but she was tired and cold, too.

The cottage was abandoned, and there was a barn out back where the unicorns could shelter. Inside, the Riders built a fire, using leftover wood sitting beside the front door.

Ellabeth huddled by the fire while the others went to sleep. She tried staying awake, but before long she had drifted off into a dream-filled sleep.

She woke in the morning feeling cozy and warm. Quinn was in the kitchen making a breakfast of hot chocolate, fruit, and boiled eggs. Krystal stood at the window looking out.

Ellabeth sat up. "Oh dear. I must have drifted off for a few minutes," she said.

"More like a few hours," Krystal laughed. "You've been snoring your head off."

"I don't snore!" said Ellabeth.

"Oh, yes you do," Krystal replied.

Ellabeth bit her tongue, refusing to be drawn into an argument. It was embarrassing enough that she had been caught napping. She had overslept, and that did nothing to help her friends feel confident in her abilities as Head Rider.

"I'm going to check on Fayza," said Ellabeth. She rose, slipping the porta-viewer into her coat pocket so the others wouldn't see.

"Breakfast will be ready soon," Quinn said.

Fayza nickered in greeting as Ellabeth walked into the barn. Ellabeth patted her absently as she took out the porta-viewer.

Although she had told Krystal and Quinn they would go through Shanahan, she still wasn't sure it was the best thing to do. All night, she'd had nightmares about black mist.

*If I use the porta-viewer, does that make me a failure?* she wondered. *Does Willow ever doubt herself like this?*

"What should I do, girl?" Ellabeth asked as she nuzzled Fayza's neck. "Part of me wants to do this on my own. But another part of me is so afraid of failing. This mission isn't just about me. It's about protecting Princess Serafina. She's Avamay's future, after all."

Fayza nudged Ellabeth's arm gently.

"You're right," Ellabeth sighed. "And so is Krystal. I should talk to Willow."

Ellabeth slid the porta-viewer open and peered into the glass. She clicked the button. The glass misted, and then Willow appeared.

"Oh, you're awake," Ellabeth said. "I thought it might be too early."

"I didn't sleep very well last night," Willow said. Her face was pale.

"How's the leg?" Ellabeth asked.

"On the mend," said Willow.

"Is Obecky's magic helping at all?" asked Ellabeth.

"It's relieving most of the pain, but it still takes time for a break to heal," Willow said. "Anyway, enough about me. What's up?"

Now that she was here, Ellabeth wasn't sure what to say. "I just wanted to see how you were," she lied.

"It's nice of you to care," Willow said as she smiled kindly. "But what's the *real* reason you contacted me?"

"Because I need your help," Ellabeth admitted.

"With what?" asked Willow.

"We've been warned by a fortune teller not to go through Shanahan because it's too dangerous," Ellabeth explained. "But if we detour around the woods, we'll be delayed, and we won't make it back to Keydell in time. What would you do, Willow?"

Willow frowned, deep in thought. "Can Fayza's magic help you travel faster if you go around the woods?" she asked.

"Usually, yes, but I relied heavily on her magic to get through last night's snowstorm," said Ellabeth. "She's already exhausted."

"It sounds risky going through Shanahan," Willow said. "I'm not there to see for myself what it's really like. You might have to work this one out on your own."

"But how?" asked Ellabeth.

"Listen to your heart and you'll know," Willow replied.

*Listen to my heart? How does that help?* Ellabeth thought.

She nodded slowly, pretending to understand. "Okay. Well, I'd better let you go," Ellabeth said. "Thanks."

She snapped the porta-viewer shut, feeling as confused as ever.

# • CHAPTER 6 •

THE RIDERS SET OUT after breakfast. It had stopped snowing. The sun was shining, and it was too hot to wear their coats. Ellabeth continued to struggle over which path they should take. By midday, they had reached the edge of the woods where the road split in two. Just as Delphi had said, one path led directly through Shanahan. The other skirted the woods and led westward to Merroweed.

Ellabeth halted Fayza, and the others stopped beside her.

Ellabeth tried doing as Willow had told her, to listen to her heart. She closed her eyes and listened hard.

But she couldn't hear anything.

"I don't know what to do," Ellabeth said.

"But I thought you wanted to go through Shanahan," Krystal said.

"I did," she admitted. "Now I'm not sure."

"If you want my advice, I think we should go around," Krystal said.

"What about you, Quinn?" Ellabeth asked.

"Whatever you decide," Quinn said. "I trust your judgement."

*How can she trust my judgement when I don't?* Ellabeth wondered.

The safer option was through Merroweed. They all knew that. Shanahan and its mist could only lead to danger. But they didn't have time for anything else.

"What if the tales Delphi and the innkeeper told us are superstitions?" Ellabeth said. "We have the unicorns, and we have each other. If we stick together and stay strong, we can do this. Will you follow me?"

"I will," Quinn said.

Ellabeth looked at Krystal. "You're Head Rider," Krystal said, "and we ride as one."

Ellabeth smiled. Finally, Krystal seemed to be supporting her. "You're right," said Ellabeth. "We do ride as one. Let's go."

Before Fayza had taken a step, however, Quinn grasped Ellabeth's arm. "Ula just sent me a mind-message," Quinn said. "She said to watch out for the golden path."

"All right, we'll keep an eye out for it," said Ellabeth.

"And avoid it," Krystal said.

Ellabeth laughed nervously. "Right," she replied.

The girls trotted single file along the path into the woods. Tall trees reached toward the sky, wild orchids hanging from their branches. Tendrils of purple, crimson, lemon, and fuchsia flowers dangled all around them, their scent flooding the forest.

"This place is beautiful," Krystal breathed, staring all around her.

"It sure is," Ellabeth agreed, wondering how such a beautiful place could be considered so dangerous. "Maybe Delphi and her bones were wrong."

"I sure hope so," said Quinn.

"Hey, who pulled my hair?" Krystal asked as she looked around.

"You probably caught it on a branch," Ellabeth said. "This path is narrow."

"Ouch! Someone is pulling *my* hair," Quinn wailed, "and it hurts."

Ellabeth glanced back at the others.

They were gone.

Ellabeth's pulse surged. "Krystal? Quinn?" she said, trying not to panic. Then, as suddenly as they had vanished, the girls reappeared.

Ellabeth rubbed her eyes. "I thought you'd gone for a second," she said.

"We thought *you'd* gone," Krystal said. "I've got the strangest feeling. . . ."

"Ula says something isn't right," Quinn said as Ula pawed the ground.

"Stay calm," Ellabeth said, as much to herself as the others. "We were warned this is an enchanted forest."

"You just said there was nothing to worry about," Krystal countered.

"Maybe there isn't," said Ellabeth. "Maybe there's a logical explanation for everything."

"Okay, so how do you explain that?" Krystal asked in a frightened voice. She pointed ahead to a thick, black mass swimming through the trees toward them.

"What is that?" Ellabeth asked. She squinted to see better. "A swarm of bees?"

"It looks like a cloud," Quinn said.

"That's not a cloud," Krystal said. "That's mist. *Black* mist."

"The Mists of Shanahan!" Ellabeth gasped.

"Let's turn back now, while we have the chance," Krystal said, her voice rising in panic.

"Nonsense," Ellabeth said. "We have the unicorns and their magic to help us. Fayza, I know you're tired, but can you please try your best to use your light magic?"

Fayza obeyed her Rider, immediately sending golden sparks of magic shooting from her horn. The sparks swirled and united in the air, forming a lit path through the black mist.

The Riders continued through the forest. All around them the black mist churned and twisted. Lightning flashed and thunder clapped all around them. Estrella, who hated storms, skittered nervously through the trees. The sounds of animals growling, hooting, and howling filled the air. Laughter, loud and rough, echoed through the woods.

"Who's making that noise?" Ellabeth shouted.

"More like *what's* making that noise," Krystal replied. "I bet there are dangerous animals out there."

"Or those noises could just be a trick," Quinn said.

The black mist began to overpower Fayza's light. It was impossible to see the path. Ellabeth wasn't even sure they were traveling in the right direction.

She rubbed her forehead, trying to think.

*Stay calm,* she told herself. *Everything will be fine.*

The air grew colder, and the sky darkened further. Ellabeth shivered. "It's freezing," she said. She pulled her coat out of her backpack and put it on. The others put their coats on, too.

"I think you're right, Quinn," Ellabeth said. "This mist is playing tricks on us."

Though she hated admitting it, Ellabeth was scared. Not only for herself, but for the unicorns and her friends. She'd put everyone in danger, and she couldn't see a way out.

"Maybe it's not too late to turn back?" Quinn suggested.

By now Ellabeth was so anxious, she didn't know which way was back. None of them did.

*What should I do?* she wondered. *What would Willow do?*

# ● CHAPTER 7 ●

LISTEN TO YOUR HEART.

The words came to Ellabeth automatically.

*That's what Willow would do,* she realized. *She would listen to her heart.*

Ellabeth tried it now. She listened hard and the words came to her.

*Ask for help.*

Ellabeth pulled the porta-viewer from her backpack and opened it up.

"Hello, Ellabeth!" Willow said, waving cheerily. Ellabeth could see she was sitting in the garden wrapped up in a blanket while Obecky grazed nearby. "How is everything going?"

"Not so good," Ellabeth said. She tried to keep her voice steady so Willow wouldn't worry too much. "We're lost in the Mists of Shanahan."

"Oh, dear," said Willow. "Do you recognize any landmarks you might have passed before? Does anything look familiar?"

"No. Nothing," replied Ellabeth.

"What about the unicorn's magic?" Willow asked. "Can you use that to help?"

"Fayza's magic is pretty much exhausted from lighting our path," said Ellabeth. "The black mist is too strong for her."

"What about Ula?" Willow asked. "Can she tell you anything?"

Ellabeth turned to Quinn. "Is Ula sending you any mind-messages?" she asked.

Quinn listened for a moment. "No," she replied shaking her head. The mist is too strong for her. She can't see clearly."

"This is hopeless!" Ellabeth wailed.

"Don't say that," Willow said. "You can do this — I know it. What about Estrella? Her magic enchants. Perhaps it can enchant the enchanted woods."

"I never thought of that," Ellabeth said hopefully. "Krystal, do you think Estrella's magic could work?" she asked.

"I'm not sure. Estrella's magic usually only works on people or on animals," Krystal said, "but I'll give it a shot."

Krystal told Estrella to use her magic.

Pearly-white magical sparks began whirling from Estrella's horn. The black mist swarmed toward the sparks. Everyone held their breath, waiting to see if Estrella's magic would work.

For long moments, white battled black. The white sparks wavered under the intensity of the black mist, like a candle sputtering in a gust of wind. It looked like the black might overcome the white and smother it.

"Try harder, E," Krystal urged. "Don't give up."

Estrella doubled her magic. White sparks spun faster and faster around the black mist until the black began twirling with the white, dancing away from the Riders and through the trees.

Now the mist was gone, and sunlight shone down, filtering through the leaves. Warm rays lit a strip of yellow buttercups that seemed to lead out of the woods.

"Estrella's done it," Ellabeth said. Her body flooded with relief. "Her magic has charmed the mist away. Thanks, Willow. I think we'll be okay now," said Ellabeth.

"I knew you could do it," Willow said. She waved and was gone.

Ellabeth stowed the porta-viewer away. "Let's follow that path before it disappears," she said.

Ellabeth nudged Fayza into a gallop, eager to be out of the woods. Krystal and Estrella followed. Ula, however, refused to move.

"The buttercups!" Quinn shouted. "That's the golden path Ula warned us about."

Ellabeth tried to stop Fayza, but it was too late. The path collapsed beneath them, dragging the unicorn down with it. The ground was swallowing Fayza.

"Help!" Ellabeth called out as Fayza thrashed beneath her.

"Jump off Fayza and get to safety!" Quinn shouted.

"No! I won't leave her," replied Ellabeth.

"You're weighing her down," Krystal said. "Jump!"

Krystal was right. Ellabeth's weight wasn't helping Fayza. Reluctantly, she leaped off her unicorn and scrambled to safe ground.

Fayza kept scrambling. She whinnied in terror.

Ellabeth was in a panic. She couldn't think. She couldn't move. All she could do was watch Fayza sink lower into the earth.

Ellabeth tried to think. An idea came to her.

"Krystal, Quinn, pass me your blankets," Ellabeth said. "We'll tie them together and use the blankets like a rope to drag Fayza out. Ula and

Estrella aren't as strong as Obecky, but together they might manage."

"Tying the unicorns will hurt them," Krystal pointed out, "and weaken their powers."

"It's our only hope," said Ellabeth.

Ellabeth knotted Krystal and Quinn's blankets tightly together. She secured one end around Estrella's neck and then stretched out across the sinking soil. She wrapped the blanket around Fayza's neck, and then she looped the other end around Ula's neck.

Estrella and Ula nickered anxiously, clearly uncomfortable at being restrained.

"Walk your unicorns slowly backward," Ellabeth said. "Be careful. We don't want to strangle Fayza."

Krystal and Quinn coaxed their unicorns into action.

"Come on, E," Krystal said.

"You can do it, Ula," said Quinn. "Easy, now."

The blankets strained. Fayza squealed and squirmed. Her hooves scraped against the ground, kicking up dirt and clay.

Still she remained stuck in the earth's hold.

Ellabeth's heart beat wildly. *I can't lose Fayza,* she thought. *I can't.*

"Pull harder!" Ellabeth said.

Fayza inched forward. Ula's hooves slipped on the grass and leaves. She lost her footing. Fayza slid back into the ground.

"No!" Ellabeth said as she grabbed the blankets to help pull. Quinn and Krystal ran in beside her. Together, the unicorns and the girls tugged with all their strength.

Inch by inch, they hauled Fayza out of the soil.

"Almost there," Ellabeth puffed. "Keep going."

Moments later, Fayza lay on firm ground, weak, and trembling. Her sides heaved heavily. She blinked several times, her nostrils flaring. Then she closed her eyes, and her sides stopped moving.

"Oh, no," Ellabeth gasped. "What have I done?"

# ● CHAPTER 8 ●

ELLABETH WAS SHATTERED. BEAUTIFUL, loyal, magical Fayza was dead.

And it was all her fault.

*Why did I ever want to be Head Rider?* Ellabeth thought. *Look where it's led!*

Ellabeth dropped to her knees, hugging Fayza's lifeless body and sobbing hot tears of despair. Krystal and Quinn looked on, their eyes wide with shock, and tears streaming down their faces.

Ula stood, her head bowed with despair and exhaustion. Estrella walked up to Fayza and sniffed her body. She snorted several times then let out a long, mournful whinny that echoed through the woods.

Lost in their misery, the sad little group didn't notice the black mist returning. Nor did they see it form into human and animal shapes around them.

"We're sorry," the mist shapes spoke as one. "We were only playing. We were only having fun. We didn't mean to harm anyone."

"What?" Krystal fumed. "Now you're talking?"

Ellabeth lifted her head. Her cheeks were stained with dust and tears. Her eyes were cold and hard. She was no longer afraid of the mist. Now she felt angry.

She climbed to her feet. "You call this playing?" Ellabeth said.

"We have so few people to play with," the mist shapes said. "No one comes into the woods anymore."

"Is it any wonder?" Ellabeth said. "You hounded us, confused us, and terrified us! Your games are dangerous and deadly. And now you've killed Fayza! How dare you destroy something so beautiful, so important to Avamay?"

"We didn't know. Our game was just for show," the mist shapes said. "We're so lonely and bored, and we don't like being ignored." The mist shapes held their hands up innocently. "There's no need for weeping. She's only sleeping."

"What do you mean?" Ellabeth demanded.

"Not dead, but sleeping," said the mist shapes. "Not dead, but . . . sleeping."

Ellabeth brushed away her tears, her heart aching with hope. She took a deep breath and drew herself up with a fearsome look on her face.

"Listen here," Ellabeth ordered the mist shapes, "if this is some kind of game, it ends right now. The Dakkar Serpent awaits us on important business. If you don't fix what you've done immediately, I'll make sure the serpent has you scattered to the four winds."

"Yes, miss. Yes, miss," the shapes trembled. "As you wish. As you wish."

"Right. Well, get to it," Ellabeth said.

The black mist was soon replaced with golden mist. It whirled around Fayza, slowly at first, but then faster. It wove through Fayza's mane, around her neck, and into her nostrils and mouth. The unicorn's eyes opened. She struggled to her feet and then shook herself all over.

"Fayza," Ellabeth said hugging her. "You're alive!"

"She's alive. She's alive," the mist shapes said.

"Enough," Ellabeth snapped. The mist shapes froze. "Now, you will lead us out of the woods and to Dakkar safely. It's the least you can do."

"Yes, miss. Yes, miss," the shapes chanted again. "As you wish. As you wish."

Bowing, the shapes set out. The Unicorn Riders followed.

"Well done, Ellabeth," Quinn said. "I bet you're the first person to tame that wicked mist in a while."

Ellabeth shuddered as she thought of how close she'd come to losing Fayza. "I only wish I'd never brought us here," Ellabeth said.

The Riders left the dark woods and the mist behind them. Blue sky returned overhead. Despite the snow elsewhere, the sun shone brightly here, and birds twittered in the trees. Fine, pale pink sand stretched out before them until it reached a shimmering, emerald lake. In the middle of the lake sat an island covered in rocks and palm trees.

Along the far curve of the lake, rocky cliffs reached toward the sky. The cliffs were covered in plants and vines and flowers in every color of the rainbow. In one spot, a waterfall flowed gently downward.

It was an oasis. The sand was made up of tiny pink diamonds, shed by the Dakkar Serpent and eroded over time.

"How gorgeous!" Krystal gasped.

Ellabeth's chest puffed with pride. She was relieved they had made it out of the woods, and her confidence was now growing. "I did it!' she said. "I found Dakkar. I'm not such a bad leader after all."

Krystal coughed. "Um, we don't have the diamonds yet, and we're still a long way from home," she said.

"Thanks for reminding me," Ellabeth groaned. "I bet this place is full of magic. Have you noticed how clear the sky is? And how warm it is all of a sudden?"

"I hope it isn't enchanted like the woods," Quinn said warily.

"I have a feeling it might be," Krystal murmured.

Suddenly, a great sound erupted from the trees and the cliffs. It was the call of thousands of birds singing in unison. The girls watched as the sky filled with birds of all kinds, eagles, parrots, larks, and wrens. They whirled and swooped in circles, warbling and chirping their sweet birdsong.

"They're welcoming us," Quinn shouted. "Have you ever seen or heard anything so amazing?"

After a few moments, the display ended and the birds flew back to their trees and rock crevices.

From the island in the center of the lake, three enormous black swans appeared. They stepped into the water and then swam across to where the Riders stood. They paddled to the water's edge before stepping out and walking up the beach. Each swan towered over the girls. Ellabeth stepped backward, nervously eyeing the red beaks, which she was certain could deliver a nasty nip.

One seemed to be the leader. "Honorable Riders," it said. The swan bowed his graceful neck to each of them. "I am Theelix, and this is my flock. We are the Guardians of Dakkar. To what do we owe this visit?"

"We've been sent by Queen Heart to collect the Dakkar Diamonds," Ellabeth explained. "They're needed for Princess Serafina's initiation ceremony."

"Yes," Theelix said. "We thought it might be time."

Before Ellabeth could reply, another swan stepped forward, bowing her head as she ruffled her wings. "I am Bakeera," she said. "Please sit on our backs, and we will carry you to the island. There you may speak to the Dakkar Serpent and see whether she will permit you to take the diamonds."

Ellabeth grew instantly worried. She had forgotten the serpent must *freely* hand over her diamond scales.

*How can I make the Dakkar Serpent give up her scales?* Ellabeth wondered. *I wished I'd asked Jala about that.*

 **CHAPTER 9**

"WHAT ABOUT OUR UNICORNS?" Krystal asked.

"They must wait here," Bakeera replied. "Come. Don't be afraid."

Krystal and Quinn eyed Ellabeth, who nodded. "We'll be back soon," Ellabeth told the unicorns. "Wait here."

She stepped toward Theelix. "Will you take me?" she asked.

The giant swan dropped down in the sand, allowing Ellabeth to climb onto his back where she was enveloped within silken feathers. "Hold onto my neck," Theelix instructed. "But not too tight."

Ellabeth did as she was told. Quinn climbed onto Bakeera's back, settling among her glossy feathers.

Krystal climbed onto a third swan's back, who the Riders learned was called Dresdeena.

It was impossible not to enjoy the ride, and soon all three girls were smiling. When they reached the island, however, Ellabeth's anxiety returned. Her stomach knotted with fear.

*Would the Dakkar Serpent give up her diamonds?* Ellabeth wondered.

"Stand on the greeting rock," Theelix instructed.

Ellabeth stepped onto a gray rock platform worn smooth by years of wind and rain.

"There!" Krystal cried. "I see something."

Ellabeth looked in the direction Krystal was pointing. The surface of the lake was swirling and churning. Something big was surfacing.

Ellabeth gulped. *Don't be afraid,* she thought.

A head poked through the water. It grew bigger, extending upward. Dripping with water, the Dakkar Serpent arched her enormous head over Ellabeth who cowered on the rock platform below.

Even while her knees were trembling, Ellabeth recognized that the serpent was extraordinarily beautiful. Her scales were hexagons of polished pink diamonds that glittered in the sun. Her eyes were emerald and rimmed with impossibly long lashes. Her underbelly was the color of creamy-white milk, and her long, forked tongue flicked gracefully in and out of her mouth.

"Who are you?" the serpent asked, startling Ellabeth. She thought the serpent's voice would be loud and booming or harsh and clipped. Instead, the serpent's voice was soft and musical, as if dancing in time to the gentle breeze.

Ellabeth drew on all her courage to speak

without faltering. "I'm Ellabeth, Head Unicorn Rider," she said.

The serpent twirled her long body in the water, rising higher into the air. Ellabeth had to squint into the sun to look at her. "You are not the Head Rider," said the serpent. "Why do you lie to me?"

"I'm s-s-sorry," Ellabeth stammered, all confidence lost. "I, er, Willow the actual Head Rider broke her leg. She couldn't come with us, so I took over."

"A great leader you showed yourself to be," said the serpent. "You almost got yourself and your friends killed in the woods."

Ellabeth winced. "Did you see that?" she asked.

"I see everything. I *know* everything," the serpent replied.

Ellabeth glanced at Krystal and Quinn. They looked even more terrified of the Dakkar Serpent than she was. If that was possible.

"I was only trying my best," Ellabeth mumbled, feeling embarrassed. It was bad enough with Krystal criticizing her all the time. She didn't need the serpent telling her what a terrible job she was doing.

"Perhaps you should try harder. Hmm?" said the serpent. "Now, tell me, what are you here for, Hummingbird Girl?" The serpent flicked her tongue at the symbol on Ellabeth's uniform.

Ellabeth's exhaustion got the best of her, and she snapped before she could stop herself. "It's Princess Serafina's initiation ceremony," she said. "We need your diamonds to make her ceremonial armor. If you know everything, surely you would know that."

The Dakkar Serpent shook her head from side to side. "How you were ever chosen to be Head Rider, even for a short time, is beyond me," said the serpent.

"I cannot entrust the Dakkar Diamonds to one who is not respectful," said the serpent. "Leave now before you make me angry." The serpent stretched out her neck so her face was inches from Ellabeth's. "And you don't want to make me angry. I assure you, it is not a pretty sight."

# • CHAPTER 10 •

"WHAT ARE WE GOING to do now?" Krystal asked.

After Ellabeth's terrible meeting with the serpent, the swans had brought the girls back to the sandy shore.

"We can't leave without the diamonds," Ellabeth said. "Princess Serafina needs them."

"The serpent told us to leave," Krystal said. "I for one don't want to disobey her. Did you see how big she is?"

"She's probably fine once you get to know her," Quinn said, trying to be helpful.

Ellabeth and Krystal stared at her in disbelief.

"Well, I mean, perhaps once you get on her good side . . .," Quinn said.

"I doubt she *has* a good side," Krystal said, pacing the shoreline.

"We're not leaving," Ellabeth said. "I just need to figure out what to do."

Krystal folded her arms. "You'd better hurry up," she said. "We're running out of time."

"Do you have to keep reminding me? I could use a little support here," Ellabeth said.

"We do support you," Krystal replied. "We work well together, except when you're bossing us around or snapping at us. A good Head Rider doesn't do that. She respects everyone on her team."

"What would you know about being Head Rider?" Ellabeth demanded. "You've never been one."

"I know how Willow treats us. She'd never act like this," Krystal sighed. "Forget it — I'm sick of arguing. I'm going for a walk."

"Don't wander too far away. You never know what might be out there," Ellabeth said. "We heard all sorts of animal sounds on the way here, remember."

Krystal groaned as she marched off. "It's an oasis. How bad can it be?" she said.

Ellabeth plopped down in the sand. She wanted to cry so badly, but crying wasn't Head Rider behavior.

Quinn crouched beside Ellabeth, sifting the sand through her hands as she spoke. "Don't worry," Quinn said. "We'll figure out something."

"How?" Ellabeth said, turning to Quinn. "I've ruined everything. I put us in danger in the forest. I insulted the Dakkar Serpent. I'm a complete failure."

"Ellabeth," Quinn gasped, "you're not a failure. You're a Unicorn Rider. You're always telling us we should be proud of who we are. Unicorn Riders can do anything. Remember?"

"It's one thing to be a Rider," Ellabeth said. She knew Quinn was right, but somehow

87

admitting it was too hard. "But being *Head* Rider is another thing altogether. All this responsibility to be the perfect leader is just too much."

"We don't expect you to be perfect," Quinn said as she studied her closely. "I don't get it. You're usually so confident. What's changed?"

"I don't know," said Ellabeth. "Ever since I became temporary Head Rider, it's like I don't believe in myself. I'm so afraid of failing. I just seize up inside. Or I push people away like I've done with Krystal. What's Queen Heart going to think when we fail this mission and the princess is the first royal in history who doesn't have magical armor? I'll never be able to look her in the eye again."

"I believe in you," Quinn said smiling. She brushed the sand off her hands and stood up. "Perhaps you should, too. Now, it's starting to get dark. I'm going to light a fire so we can eat. You need to use that sharp brain of yours to figure out how we're going to get those diamonds."

Ellabeth watched Quinn as she marched off. *Maybe she's right,* she thought. *Maybe it is time I started believing in myself.*

Later that night, the others were asleep in their sleeping bags, but Ellabeth was wide awake. She still hadn't figured out how she might convince the serpent to give them her precious scales. Time was slipping away.

Ellabeth crept silently past Quinn and Krystal. A gentle nicker made her stop.

"Fayza," Ellabeth whispered. "Can't you sleep either?" Fayza nuzzled her shoulder. "Walk with me then."

Together, Ellabeth and Fayza slipped down to the water's edge. The moon was huge and white, making the lake shine in the darkness.

Ellabeth sat down and pulled out the porta-viewer. She hoped Willow wouldn't mind her getting in touch so late. She flicked the porta-viewer open and clicked the button. The glass shimmered then cleared.

Willow was sitting up in bed, her short hair tousled as she rubbed her eyes. "Ellabeth? Is that you?" Willow asked.

"Yes," Ellabeth whispered. "Sorry to wake you. I know it's late."

"No problem," Willow said. "What's up?"

"How's your leg?" Ellabeth asked.

"Jala says it's healing well. Did you want to talk about something?" Willow asked.

"Yes," Ellabeth replied. "It's just, well, I badly wanted to be Head Rider, but this mission has been so hard."

"When aren't our missions hard?" Willow chuckled.

"I guess you're right," Ellabeth sighed, "but I've made so many mistakes."

"Making mistakes is part of learning," Willow said kindly.

"This latest mistake is a *huge* one," Ellabeth said. She told Willow what had happened with the Dakkar Serpent. "What should I do?" she asked Willow.

"What is your heart telling you?" Willow replied.

Ellabeth listened hard. Harder than she had ever listened before. The answer soon came to her.

"Apologize?" asked Ellabeth.

"I think you knew the answer all along," Willow said. "You really didn't need me."

"Thanks, Willow. I see now why you're such a good Head Rider," said Ellabeth. "I hope we'll be home soon. I miss you."

"I miss you girls, too," Willow said. "Good luck."

Ellabeth closed the porta-viewer and stood up.

She had to find the Dakkar Serpent.

# • CHAPTER 11 •

ELLABETH WANDERED ALONG THE shoreline with Fayza. There was no sign of the guardians. If she wanted to speak to the serpent she would have to swim to the island. The thought of getting into the dark water where the serpent was, scared Ellabeth. But she had to do it for the good of the mission.

"Girl, use your magic," Ellabeth whispered. "Light up the water for me."

Golden sparks leaped from Fayza's topaz horn, swirling over the water. The sparks attracted fireflies, and the air lit up with glowing bugs.

For a short time, Ellabeth forgot her troubles, wondering at the beauty of the nighttime scene. It glowed like a rainbow at night.

The sound of leaves rustling caught Ellabeth's attention. She told Fayza to stop her magic. Then she tiptoed cautiously toward the trees. Parting the ferns, Ellabeth peered in and saw a group of large, pink eggs sitting in a nest of soft sand. One of the eggs was moving.

Ellabeth realized the eggs were the serpent's, and one of them was about to break open. A baby serpent was hatching.

The egg wobbled again. A tiny crack appeared in the shell, then grew longer. The shell burst open, and a baby serpent pushed its way out. The baby blinked and chirped happily. It was a perfect, tiny imitation of its mother.

*Where is its mother?* Ellabeth wondered, glancing nervously over her shoulder.

Just then, a deep rumbling came from the bushes nearby. A pair of olive green eyes glowed at Ellabeth through the darkness.

Leopard eyes.

Ellabeth picked up a stick that had been lying on the ground. "Stay close to me, girl," she instructed Fayza.

The leopard crept slowly out of the bushes and toward the eggs and baby serpent. It bared its teeth, prowling closer.

Ellabeth leaped out from her hiding spot. She ran between the leopard and the baby serpent, waving her stick. "Go away!" she yelled.

The leopard flinched, but when it saw she was only a girl, it snarled fiercely. It wasn't going to give up its meal without a fight.

The leopard and Ellabeth circled each other.

Ellabeth's pulse pounded in her throat.

*I must stand firm,* Ellabeth told herself. *I can't let anything happen to these babies.*

Fayza nickered uncertainly. Ellabeth motioned to her to stay still.

With a throaty roar, the leopard bounded toward her. Ellabeth braced herself and remembered her training. Legs apart, stick held ready. When the leopard sprang toward her, Ellabeth flicked one end of her stick upward. She whacked the animal hard under its chin. The leopard's head snapped backward, but it still managed to land on all fours.

The baby serpent screeched and darted between Ellabeth's feet for protection. Growling furiously, the leopard bounded toward Ellabeth again.

"Use your magic, Fayza!" Ellabeth shouted.

Fayza's golden magic shot from her horn, blinding the leopard as it pounced. Ellabeth whacked the beast on its chest and rear and sent it flying backward.

Between the fearsome girl, her stick, and the fiery light burning above the unicorn's head, the leopard knew it had been beaten. With a snarl of disapproval, it retreated into the trees.

Panting and shaking, Ellabeth threw her stick to the ground. Fayza trotted over and nuzzled her shoulder. Ellabeth bent to pick up the baby serpent, cooing to it softly and making sure it was okay.

Quinn and Krystal burst into the clearing. "Ellabeth, is everything all right? We heard a terrible roar," they said.

"Leopard," Ellabeth said, still in shock. "Baby." She held the tiny serpent out for Krystal and Quinn to admire.

"Well, well." Ellabeth heard a voice behind them. "What have we here?" said the voice.

Ellabeth turned, her eyes wide with fear. Denying a leopard a meal was one thing, trying to explain

to a gigantic mother serpent why she was holding her baby was something else.

"I was . . .," Ellabeth started to say. Her mouth was so dry she couldn't speak.

"Ellabeth saved your babies," Krystal said. "She fought off a leopard."

Ellabeth smiled gratefully at Krystal. Despite their differences, Ellabeth realized she could still rely on Krystal.

"I saw," the serpent said. "And I thank you most sincerely." Her forked tongue flicked out to tickle her baby's chin. Ellabeth set the wriggling creature on the ground. It slithered over to its mother. "I thought I told you to leave, Hummingbird Girl?" said the serpent.

"I can't leave," Ellabeth said as she bowed her head. "Leaving would mean failing my mission."

"You're a stubborn little thing, aren't you?" replied the serpent.

"I like to think of it as determined," Ellabeth said.

"Certainly, your bravery is undeniable," said the serpent. "You have surprised me." The serpent turned to Quinn and Krystal. "Do you mind if Ellabeth and I speak alone?"

"Sure," Krystal said. "We'll be up the beach."

"Will you be okay?" Quinn asked, looking worried.

"I'll be fine," Ellabeth said. She wandered down to the water with the serpent and her baby. The sun was just beginning to rise. The birds were waking, greeting the new day with their song.

"I'm sorry I got angry earlier," Ellabeth said. She peeked shyly at the huge creature to check her reaction.

"Go on," the serpent said, gliding across the sand as Ellabeth walked beside her.

"I have a habit of rushing in without thinking," Ellabeth continued, "and this mission means an awful lot to me and to Princess Serafina. I've never been Head Rider before, and I really want to return home with the Dakkar Diamonds. For the first time ever, I'll be able to prove to Queen Heart, my father, and everyone else that I'm somebody."

"You *are* somebody," the serpent said. "You're a Unicorn Rider. You should be content with that."

"Oh, I am," said Ellabeth. "It's just, I always feel I have something to prove. To show people I'm not some boring farmer's daughter from Cardamon."

"I have a feeling no one has ever thought of you as boring," said the serpent chuckling. "Now, look in the lake, Hummingbird Girl."

As Ellabeth gazed out at the water, an image of her father appeared.

"Papa!" she said.

"Remember that we will always love you, Beth," said her father's reflection. "Your star will shine brighter than any you see in the sky."

"He said that the last time I saw him," Ellabeth said quietly. She was close to tears. "How did you do that?"

"I told you, I see everything," the serpent replied. "And I hear everything. Even what is in here." Her tongue flicked out to touch Ellabeth's heart. "Your father is proud of you. He would be even if you weren't a Unicorn Rider. If you listened to your heart, you would know it's true."

"Willow told me to listen to my heart, too," said Ellabeth.

"Perhaps it's time you took our advice. Hmm?" said the serpent. The serpent eyed Ellabeth solemnly. "Now, tell me, how many diamonds do you need?"

"Does that mean you'll give us your scales?" asked Ellabeth.

"You saved my babies," the serpent replied. "It is the least I can do."

Ellabeth was overwhelmed with relief. But then she realized they wouldn't make it back to Keydell in time for Princess Serafina's ceremony.

As if reading Ellabeth's mind, the serpent smiled. "And I have a way for you to make it home on time, too," she said.

# • CHAPTER 12 •

"CONGRATULATIONS, ELLABETH," JALA SAID. "I knew you could do it."

*I'm so glad to be home,* Ellabeth thought joyfully. *I'm so glad I didn't fail my mission.*

With the help of the Guardian Swans, the Riders and their unicorns had made it back to Keydell the previous day. The swans had each carried a Rider and a unicorn on their broad backs, though the unicorns had to stay seated for the entire flight.

The queen's seamstresses had worked through the night to complete Princess Serafina's battle armor for the ceremony at dawn.

Now Jala, Ellabeth, and the other Unicorn Riders, including Willow, were seated beside the royal family. Princess Serafina's initiation ceremony had commenced with a brilliant display of acrobatics from the queen's performers.

Ellabeth's eyes sought the three enormous guardians on the other side of the arena. The unicorns stood beside them, flicking their manes and tails from side to side occasionally.

Ellabeth allowed herself a silent chuckle. She hadn't told the others that having the swans fly them home had been the serpent's idea. The serpent had said it would be their little secret, a special gift to Ellabeth to thank her for saving her babies.

Everything was going to be all right. The Dakkar Diamonds would keep their magic. The princess would be able to take her armor with her when they traveled to the Council of Kingdoms. And it would protect her in battles to come.

"You have many qualities of a good leader," Jala said interrupting her thoughts. "Courage. Determination. Strength."

"But not others like patience, an even temper, and self-belief?" Ellabeth asked.

"You're young yet. Those skills can be learned," Jala said kindly. "If only you would believe in yourself, you could make anything happen."

Ellabeth knew Jala was right. She was also happy she wasn't Head Rider any more.

The acrobats finished their display. The crowd broke into applause, Jala and Ellabeth along with them.

"For now, it's enough to know you succeeded in this mission," Jala spoke above the applause. "You brought the Dakkar Diamonds back for Princess Serafina's initiation. The magic will hold."

"And doesn't she look stunning?" Krystal leaned in to whisper.

"Krystal," Ellabeth gasped. "Have you been eavesdropping?"

Krystal shrugged. "I couldn't help overhearing," she said.

Ellabeth studied Princess Serafina wearing her diamond armor. It would give her super strength and protect her whenever she wore it. And just as Krystal had said, it did look fabulous the way it glittered in the golden dawn sunshine.

Still, Ellabeth thought Serafina seemed nervous. The princess must have felt Ellabeth's eyes on her because she looked over at her.

Ellabeth smiled and mouthed the words, "You'll be fine."

The princess smiled shyly at Ellabeth and mouthed back, "Thanks!"

Ellabeth turned back to Krystal. "I suppose you want to say 'I told you so,' since I wasn't any good as Head Rider," said Ellabeth.

"You had your moments," Krystal said. "Some things you did were amazing. Like fighting that leopard and convincing the serpent to let the swans fly everyone home in time."

"And other things?" Ellabeth asked.

"Other things I would have done differently," Krystal replied.

"I suppose you would have," Ellabeth conceded. "We are very different, after all."

"And sometimes, you two are so similar it makes me laugh," Jala said with a twinkle in her eye.

The two girls stared at each other. "What do you mean?" they asked.

"Never you mind," Jala chuckled. "Now, girls, sit back and enjoy the ceremony. You've earned this honor."

Krystal shot Ellabeth a warm smile. Ellabeth winked back at her. Then she linked her arm through Krystal's and sat back to enjoy the ceremony.

# Glossary

**agile** (AJ-ahyl)—able to move quickly and easily

**criticize** (KRIT-i-size)—to tell someone what he or she has done wrong, often in an impatient way

**detour** (DEE-toor)—a different, usually longer way to go somewhere when the direct route is closed or blocked

**enchant** (en-CHANT)—to delight or charm someone

**excel** (ik-SEL)—to do something extremely well

**initiation** (i-NISH-ee-a-shuhn)—a ceremony in which a person is made a member of a club or group

**offend** (uh-FEND)—to make someone feel upset or angry

**pavilion** (puh-VIL-yuhn)—an open building that is used for shelter or recreation or for a show

**reflex** (REE-fleks)—an action that happens without a person's control or effort

**superstition** (soo-pur-STI-shuhn)—a belief that an action can affect the outcome of a future event

**treacherous** (TRECH-ur-uhs)—disloyal and not to be trusted

**unique** (yoo-NEEK)—one of a kind

# Discussion Questions

1. Do you think Ellabeth should have taken Delphi's advice to take the long way around the woods? Why or why not?

2. What were some things Ellabeth did throughout the book that did not show good leadership?

3. What choices and actions made Ellabeth a good leader?

# Writing Prompts

1. Ellabeth and Krystal both jumped at the chance to be Head Rider while Quinn quickly announced she was happy to let someone else lead. Which Rider are you most like and why?

2. Why do you think Ellabeth hid talking to Willow from the other Riders?

3. Ellabeth felt unsure of her decision to enter the woods. Have you ever made a decision and then wondered if it was the right thing to do? Write about it.

# UNICORN RIDERS

**COLLECT THE SERIES!**